Paula and Mr. Meanie Pants

Kristin Rowan

Published by Kristin Rowan, 2019.

PAULA AND MR. MEANIE PANTS

First edition. October 1, 2019.

ISBN: 978-0578571652

Written by Kristin Rowan.

Thank you to my wife, for her artwork and support

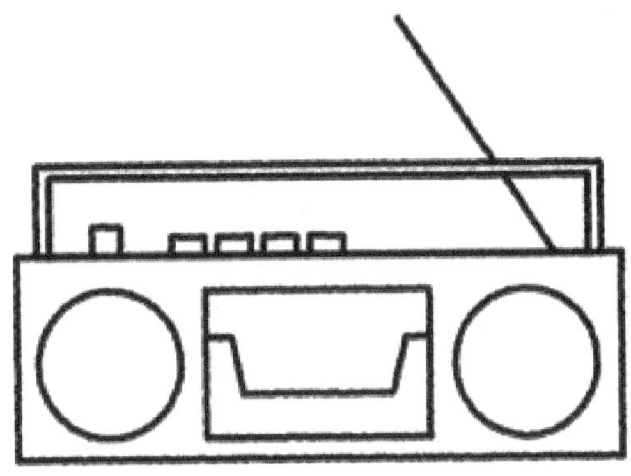

ONE

I hid in the casket, holding in giggles.

"We can take care of everything here for you," my dad said in the other room. He sounded like he could be the dad in a cartoon for grown-ups, but he used his voice to calm people down instead of saying funny things. "Let's take a look at the caskets we have available and see what you think."

I got ready to yell, "Boo!" but as my dad and the old woman came in, I started giggling more and couldn't stop.

"What is that sound?" the woman asked. I giggled still harder.

My dad sighed. "Beverly!"

I clambered out of the casket and ran back to my playroom. My father let out a deep Marge-Simpson-style groan before apologizing to the woman.

———

I set up all the toys in the playroom as my audience. I had some of my brother Ben's old dinosaur-skeleton puzzles that could stand up even though they were only bones. They were in the front row because my sister Bea's old Cabbage Patch dolls could see through them.

It was almost time for my favorite show, *Wait, Wait, Don't Tell Me*. My parents had put a radio in there for me to use. The dial was tricky, so I always just left it on OPB. I learned all sorts of things. Monica Lewinsky was hanging out at the White House even though she was not the president. Kip Kinkel brought a gun to his school and shot people.

Once the show started, I stood in the corner, which was my stage, and played all the parts. I didn't understand most of what I was saying, but the audience laughed anyway. Lots of scary-sounding things happened, but no one was scared. They especially laughed whenever I was being Paula Poundstone, because she was the funniest one.

———

In addition to being a theater, my playroom was an art gallery. I had a shoebox full of old crayons. They reminded me of that smell that happened right after it rained when it hadn't rained for a long time. Whenever I drew a picture that turned out good, I taped it up onto the wall. My mom moved some of the pictures higher to give me room to put up new pictures where I could reach.

I drew all sorts of things. I drew spaghetti, which we had for dinner a lot. I drew our minivan, which was falling apart but still worked some of the time. I drew a red train. I drew the solar system, including Pluto. I drew mailboxes and fire hydrants. I drew our dog, Suzie, who looked like Toto but my older brother named her Suzie anyway. I drew a moose, my favorite animal. I drew spiderwebs. I drew our neighbor who liked to make things and lived on the other side of our duplex. I drew the old lady from our neighborhood who walked her cat. I drew our gravedigger, Meredith, with music notes around her head because she liked to sing while she was digging.

———

It rained a lot because we lived in Boring. My parents told me that. It was close to Portland. Sometimes when it wasn't raining, my parents, Meredith, and I would all eat lunch outside together on the porch. When Meredith wasn't working, she liked to make various kinds of pie, and then she would bring the leftovers to share for lunch. Mostly, she made meat-and-vegetable pies, but sometimes she made quiches, which were basically breakfast pies. For special events, like somebody's birthday, she'd make their favorite kind of dessert pie. I got a banana cream pie every year.

One time when we were eating leftover shepherd's pie, my mom said, "So you know that actor who got in a wreck on the way to Ashland?" She was mostly talking to my dad and a little bit Meredith, but I was also there.

"Yeah," my dad said. "He was going down there to be Hamlet. That's the sort of role you die for." He sounded very proud of himself.

"Oh, honey," my mom said. "Well, while I was embalming him, I got a call from his parents, and they said that the director had given them his costume because the understudy wasn't going to be able to wear it. It would be too baggy for him. They want him to wear it for the funeral. I almost started crying because that shouldn't be the reason he's wearing it, but since he's dead, I imagine that's probably what he would want."

"Oh, that's perfect." Meredith watched as a squirrel climbed up one of the pine trees.

"It's too bad we don't keep random skulls around so he could have a Yorick," my dad said.

―――――

A little boy came into my playroom and sat in the corner, whimpering to himself. His face was all red and splotchy. He looked like he could be a friend.

"Do you want to play tic-tac-toe?" I asked. I didn't have any fancy games, but I had my shoebox of crayons and lots of scratch paper. My parents gave me all the death certificates with typos to color on.

"Sure," he said.

I drew the tic-tac-toe board with a blue crayon and gave the boy a green crayon. "Did you know that boy mooses have antlers but girl mooses don't? That's not fair! If I was a moose, I'd want antlers. Why be a moose without antlers? You would have antlers if you were a moose." I pointed at my drawing of a moose on the wall.

The boy shrugged. He didn't care that he would have a better experience as a moose than I would. I was polite and let him go first. He put an *X* on one of the sides, which was dumb. I put an *O* in the middle because sometimes when my mom didn't have to be making mummies, she'd come and play tic-tac-toe with me, and she said that was the best square if you could get it. Another thing she liked to do was sing me songs. Her favorite song was about worms:

Nobody likes me,
Everybody hates me,
Guess I'll go eat worms.
Short fat juicy ones.
Long thin slimy ones.
Itsy-bitsy, fuzzy-wuzzy worms!

That didn't help with tic-tac-toe, though. Next, the boy put another *X* on top of his first one. I knew what he was trying to do, so I put an *O* under his *X*s. He was not very focused even though he was old enough to probably be in kindergarten already. He put his next *X* next to my middle *O*, and that was pretty dumb because then I got three in a row.

Then he started crying more. "I hate you, Mr. Meanie Pants!" He shoved the shoebox of crayons off the table at me. Maybe he thought I was a boy because I had short hair, and maybe he didn't know that girls could have short hair too. The box landed upside down, and the crayons splattered everywhere.

His dad came rushing into the playroom to get him. His face was all red and splotchy too. My dad was standing behind the boy's dad, and he gave me a look like he was thinking, "Wow, what is up with him?"

I gave him a look back like I was saying, "Yeah, I know. I was being nice like I'm supposed to."

They left, and I spent the rest of the afternoon pretending the crayons were little basketballs and shooting them into the shoe-box.

———————

"Doctor, doctor give me the news," my sister Bea sang.

"You're turning into a frog," I said.

"Oh! It can't be true!"

"It is."

"Nooo!" Over the next ten minutes or so, Bea turned into a frog. She looked like a poisonous frog because she always wore bright colors. It was like she wanted to look like a pack of high-lighters. Her glasses made her look even more like a frog because they were big and round. Her hair did not make her look like a frog because it was long and curly. First she was sticking out her tongue a lot, and eventually she was hopping around the room, looking for flies.

"Well, that's obnoxious," Ben said. He was not as into babysitting me as Bea was, and he would not look like a poisonous frog if he was pretending to be a frog because he was boring.

"I guess I'll have to find my prince," Bea said. "*Ribbit*."

"The only boys here are Ben and Dennis," I said. Dennis had come over to play Monopoly with Ben, and they were both ignoring us. Ben put on one of his John Denver cassettes to help tune us out.

"Your sisters are so weird," Dennis said.

Bea played leapfrog with me until our parents got home for late dinner.

One night at an especially late dinner, my dad said, "Exciting news! Five people died today!"

The next day, we got to go to Fred Meyer, the place that had everything. Their bags of hamburger and hotdog buns only cost nineteen cents! That wasn't even their sale price. That was just how much they were. Whenever we went there, my parents always bought a ton of buns, and for the next week we'd be eating hamburger-bun pizzas and hotdog-bun sandwiches. We didn't usually eat hamburgers and hotdogs with them because the hamburgers and the hotdogs cost so much more than the buns.

While we were in the fruits-and-vegetables section, I noticed that some of the displays were kind of like little clubhouses. I crawled through the crates holding up the nectarines and sat down. I didn't get to smell nectarines very often because they cost too much money. There were people pushing carts around and chatting, but I couldn't see them.

A small dinosaur came walking up to me from the shadows. Not a pretend dinosaur—a real dinosaur, a stegosaurus. She was normal dinosaur colors, and she smelled like matcha tea. I wasn't scared because I had seen pictures of them in books.

"My name is Paula," the grocery-store dinosaur said. I hadn't been expecting her to talk, but I wasn't about to pass up this chance for friendship.

"I'm Bev. Beverly really, but most people call me Bev. Do you like listening to *Wait, Wait, Don't Tell Me?*"

"Oh, yes, I love that show."

"I wish I could live in the grocery store like you. There's so much yummy food here!"

"I don't eat most of it, though. I'm an herbivore. I only eat plants. You can tell 'cause of my teeth."

Ben had told me about how different dinosaurs had different teeth, when he was reading to me one time. Maybe if I had hidden in the meat section, I would have found a little velociraptor instead.

My dad's clomping feet were getting closer to my clubhouse. "Bev! Bev! Shit, Beverly, where are you?"

As I was crawling back out, Paula showed me a tap-dancing routine she had made up. Her feet were perfect for it with her big nails. I applauded, and she climbed into my pocket.

"Oh, phew! Beverly, what were you doing under there?" my dad asked.

"Playing with my dinosaur friend."

He paused. Then he said, "Aw, I had an imaginary friend when I was growing up too. Mine was a person, though. A dinosaur is very creative."

I didn't know what "imaginary" meant, but I thought it probably meant something like *awesome*, so I didn't argue.

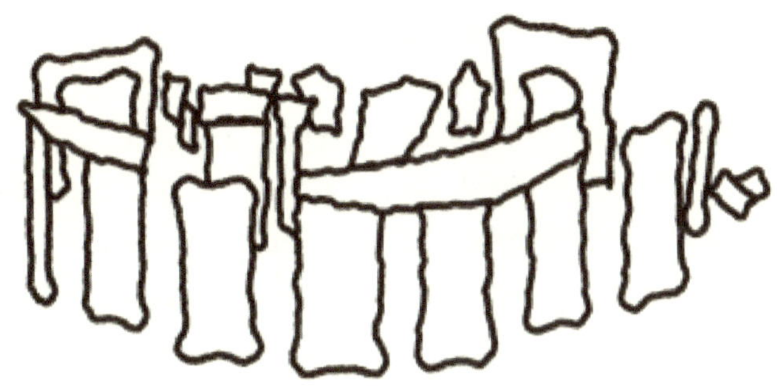

TWO

Bea and I had a desk in our room, but I preferred to sit in bed to draw or work on homework. She let me have the top bunk because she knew it was a lot more exciting to me than it would have been to her. I liked sleeping on a bunk bed because it felt like the sort of thing people leading exciting lives did. Prisoners and soldiers slept on bunk beds.

I fantasized about growing up to be a farmer so I could grow all the yummy food. One day, when I was drawing a farm, Bea burst into the room and yelled, "We're all going to die! First Columbine, and now this! The planes will fall from the sky. The computers are all going to explode. The mice will come up from the sewers, and we'll all get the bubonic plague!" She dove dramatically onto her bed and sobbed. Paula scrambled off the windowsill and hid under my pillow.

"What? What are you talking about?" I asked.

"The year 2000 is coming!"

Apparently, this was supposed to mess everything up, but I'd never been afraid of a date before, and I wasn't about to start now. Paula and I were nervous about asteroids, but I wasn't afraid of the year getting bigger. "That's just a big number, silly!"

Once Paula realized nothing scary was happening, she bounded around the room, taking breaks to pretend to be scared of random things—the dresser, the lava lamp, Bea's Backstreet Boys CD, my stuffed moose named Quentin. Bea ignored her and went over to Ben's room to discuss our impending demise.

Ben scoffed. "Computers are smarter than that."

"I think things are not really as scary as your sister thinks," Paula said.

I nodded.

———

Once I started kindergarten, there were lots of people who could be my friend. One day, Millie and I were the first two to finish the assignment, which meant we were the first two kids allowed to play. Millie always had her hair in a braid and wore button-up shirts even though we didn't have to be fancy at school.

Paula noticed her playing in the block area and said, "You should go play with her." So I went up to Millie, who was standing some blocks up in a circle.

"Are you making a stadium?" I asked.

"No."

"A circle?"

"No."

"What is it?" I asked.

"Stonehenge."

"What's that?"

"A place grown-ups go to look around and go like this..." She sighed like she was thinking about something really important. "They think about stuff."

"Are there dead people there?" I asked. "Grown-ups think about stuff a lot when someone dies, and they don't really know what to do sometimes. My mom said it's kind of like a chicken with its head cut and you have to hug it and say, 'It's okay. You can still lay eggs, even without a head. You can still be a chicken.'"

"No, it's just alive people who like looking at big rocks. And there's no chickens there because it's not a farm."

I helped her build it some more, and then we walked around it and pretended to think about stuff. I was pretending to think about the stock market. It was fun until Jake finished his work and came over and destroyed Stonehenge.

"We were still using that," I said.

Millie started crying.

"Nu-uh! You weren't touching it! That means it's not yours!" Jake yelled.

"That's not what that means. I still have things I'm not touching. I'm not touching my family, and I still have them—they just don't go to this school because they're old and they go to older-kid school, and my parents have to go to work to make money, but they're still mine. And I'm not touching my toy microphone because it's at home, and I don't—"

Our teacher interrupted me and made us clean everything up and find something else to do because she said we weren't getting along, but really, we *were* getting along except for Jake. Paula scurried back into my purple plastic lunch box. She liked to hang out in there while I was at school.

——————

Millie and I went to Tickle Creek sometimes to skip rocks. Neither of us could really do it, though, so really, we were just throwing rocks in the water. She didn't talk very much, but she did see a duck, and then she said, "Hey, a duck." It was nice of her because I hadn't seen the duck, and then I did get to see the duck.

I was on the lookout for bears. "I can never remember with bears if you're supposed to curl up in a ball and act tiny or stand up and act really scary. I might be too tiny to be scary even if I was trying to act big. It would be hard not to run away, but then the bear might think I was playing and run after me and eat me, like, as a game. Bears don't even like eating humans, I don't think, because we're not salmon. If only I was a moose, I wouldn't have to be scared of bears because I'd be big and majestic, and the bears would probably just want to be my friend."

Millie shrugged. I could tell she liked me, though. We threw a few more rocks in the water before trudging home.

——————

In second grade, Millie and I made up a secret language inspired by Helen Keller, so that we could communicate with each other using just the fingers on one hand. We didn't do it the same way Helen Keller did, because her way seemed confusing. Really, we just drew the letters into each other's hands.

Some letters were really easy to get mixed up like *U, V,* and *Y.* We fixed that by pushing down really hard at the bottom of the *V.* With the *Y,* we pushed down really hard with the line at the bottom. We didn't even have to *talk* when we talked.

Most of the time that we finger spelled together in class, we were being good and talking about the books we were supposed to read, because most of the class did not actually read the books. They were missing out on *Charlotte's Web, Winnie-the-Pooh, Phantom Tollbooth, Charlie and the Chocolate Factory, Stuart Little,* and lots of other good books.

"*T-H-E-Y A-C-T L-I-K-E R-E-A-L A-M-I-N-A-L-S B-U-T T-H-E-R-E N-O-T,*" Millie fingered to me once. She had to do it a few times before I could figure out what she was saying. Our class had just finished reading *Winnie-the-Pooh.*

"*Y-E-A-H I-F-O-R-G-E T T-H-E-Y A-R-E S-T-U-F-I-E-S,*" I replied.

It was a shame that Paula didn't have fingers. She just had to sit quietly in my pocket and listen to the other children's poor excuse for a literary discussion. "This book had too many pages," Jake complained once. I could feel Paula sigh in my pocket.

———

That winter, there was enough snow to cancel school for a few days, and our heater broke too. We all wore sweaters and sweatshirts inside. We drank lots of tea even when we weren't thirsty. Oolong was my favorite.

Paula enjoyed pretending she was a dragon because we could see our breath inside. Ben stayed in his room most of the time, working on college applications. Our parents bundled up and walked to work so they wouldn't have to drive. Bea talked to her friends on the phone a bunch and played legos with me a little bit.

It took a few days, but eventually, the repairman came to fix our heater. He wore his jumpsuit, a heavy jacket, and his toolbelt. It only took him a few hours, and then it was fixed.

"That's what you should do when you grow up," Paula said.

"I don't know how to fix anything."

The repairman didn't let us in the room to watch him, but we could hear his tools clanging through the door.

"You could learn, and then you could wear a toolbelt and be important too."

"That would be fun."

—————

My parents gave me a chore to do after school, which was to stop at the bakery outlet. It was kind of on my way home, and I liked walking anyway. They had a special where if you spent at least five dollars, you could pick out an item from the free shelf, so my parents sent me there with six dollars. My goal was to spend over five dollars but as close to five dollars as I could. I was also keeping quantity of food in mind. I brought a piece of paper to write the prices down on to keep track.

I got a loaf of white bread because that was what I liked and three loaves of wheat bread because that was what everyone else liked. It was okay to get lots of bread because we could put it in the freezer for later. Each loaf was eighty-nine cents. I skipped the bun aisle because it was cheaper to get those at Fred Meyer. I was also tired of buns. I got everything bagels that cost $1.29.

Then I was kind of stuck because that all added up to $4.85, so I had to get something else. I saw a loaf of sourdough bread that I wanted on the free shelf. The cookies were all, like, two dollars, so that wasn't going to work. I paced through the store, pondering.

I ended up putting back one of the wheat breads and getting some cinnamon raisin English muffins for $1.29, same as the bagels. That added up to $5.25, which meant I could get the sourdough bread for free.

————

Our teachers in elementary school were really into cursive writing for some reason. Paula liked to peek over the edge of my desk and watch me write. "It's like your pencil is dancing," she remarked once in class. She mimicked how the pencil was moving, so I bopped her on the head gently with it because she was distracting me.

Millie hated cursive, and whenever we got an assignment, she would raise her hand and ask, "Does it have to be in cursive?" It was the only time she would ever talk in class, which proved how much she disliked cursive. It became the thing that all our classmates knew her for.

Sometimes our teacher would be nice, but for the most part, the answer was, "Yes, Millie, it has to be in cursive." This conversation happened so often that eventually the whole class would join in with the answer.

"Yes, Millie, it has to be in cursive," the class would repeat as if they weren't hoping for the same thing.

—————

There was another thing that Millie was known for at school, and that was that she would run like a horse instead of like a kid. She'd move one leg forward and then move the other one up to it, and that was how horses galloped, she said. She really liked horses. I didn't know how to run like one, so when we ran the mile in gym class, I just ran it in a normal way. We were the last two to finish, but she was almost always faster than I was.

—————

Ben left to go study at the University of Michigan. When he came back to visit us, he told us about how busy he was with all of his homework. He was studying history. The next time he came home, he brought his girlfriend to visit.

When Ben left, Bea moved into his old bedroom, and I got a room all to myself. I could sleep on the top bunk or the bottom bunk. Paula slept on whichever one I wasn't on so I wouldn't get too lonely. It was fun having my own room during the daytime, but at nighttime, it was too quiet.

—————

Whenever Millie and I would hang out at her house, we liked to put on fake fancy-dinner parties. She had a nice dining room for it. That part wasn't fake. They had a large glass-doored cabinet full of expensive plates and cups to look at for fun. We weren't al-lowed to play with them, though, because they were worth "more than both of our lives combined," according to her mother. The table and twelve chairs were slippery-looking dark-brown wood. Millie's family even had a chandelier instead of a regular light. My family got most of our things from estate sales. Our mugs and stuff were all mismatched. We also got a lot of our clothes from those sales. Millie's dad worked from home in the office, but I only knew that because she told me. He never came out.

To make our pretend party extra fancy, we would both try to speak in fancy British accents. "You fohrgot the second fohrk! You need a second fohrk for the salad!" she would yell.

I didn't see the need for multiples of the same kind of utensil for the same meal, but I did it anyway because she knew better than I did what fancy dinners were supposed to look like. She had the heaviest silverware I had ever seen. Paula tried to lift one of the soup spoons and couldn't. She panted like a cartoon character and wiped some sweat off her forehead.

I collected a bunch of Millie's fanciest-looking stuffies to sit in some of the chairs. We had Mr. Stuffington the teddy bear, Ms. Paddy the raccoon, Señor Pasta the doll, Polka Dot the flamingo, Nicholas the hippo, and Joe the dog. They were all very polite, but none of them were good conversationalists. They also didn't really eat anything, but that was all just as well because the food was fake.

We sipped our pretend chardonnay and chatted about our days until her mom got home and it was time for them to get ready for their real fancy dinner. I imagined they would eat steak and asparagus.

———

Sometimes when Millie and I were walking home from school together, we would stop at the McDonald's to get McFlurries. Millie would always buy my McFlurry for me—Oreo, of course. "You bought them last time! Now it's my turn to buy them!" She'd say that every time so if anyone was paying attention, they wouldn't judge me.

Often, as I'd get home, our neighbor would be out on his porch on his side of the duplex, using his pottery wheel. His yard was full of things he'd made, like pots, metal sculptures, birdhouses, and painted rocks.

"What a beautiful day, huh, Beverly?" he said once. "The sun is shining, and there you are, eating magical snow with candy in it." I never knew what to say to him. Plus, Oreos weren't candy. They were cookies.

———

I was trying to race Millie on a math assignment while Jake, the most annoying but also cutest boy in fifth grade, was sitting behind me. A nice thing about going to a small school was that Millie was always in the same class as me, but so was Jake. By fifth grade, Jake had spiky hair with little blond highlights on the tips, which only added to his annoyingness. He looked like he wanted to be in a boy band like the ones Bea's friends liked. He would have fit right in with one of the posters in her room.

Every few minutes, Jake would poke my shoulder, and when I turned around, he would act like he hadn't done anything. I wasn't stupid, though. I knew he was poking me. I was falling further and further behind in the race. The sixth time he did it, I'd finally had enough. I stood up and walked the two steps back to his desk with my hands clenched.

"Beverly?" Ms. Waples said from behind her desk full of apples.

I didn't have a plan. I looked at Jake's fake-confused face. I wasn't sure what type of expression could have made me angrier. Paula slept through the whole thing in my lunch box.

"Beverly, are you all right?" our teacher asked. Her chair legs screeched across the floor as she stood up.

I was running out of time. I threw my arm at Jake's dumb spiky hair, grabbed it, and pulled it as hard as I could. He yelped like a basset hound.

Ms. Waples pulled me away from him and made me sit by myself in the hallway. He should have been the one in the hallway! I did my best to stop shaking from how angry I felt. I could have probably been a better teacher than her, even though I hadn't been to teaching school.

I complained to Millie on our walk home. "I didn't want to be the one to punish him! Stupid Ms. Waples! She didn't leave me any choice!"

"That's why I don't like people," she said. "One time, this boy kept untying my shoe, and he wouldn't stop, and I said I was going to tell my mom, so later I did, and she said it was okay because he was just doing it 'cause he likes me."

"That's so dumb."

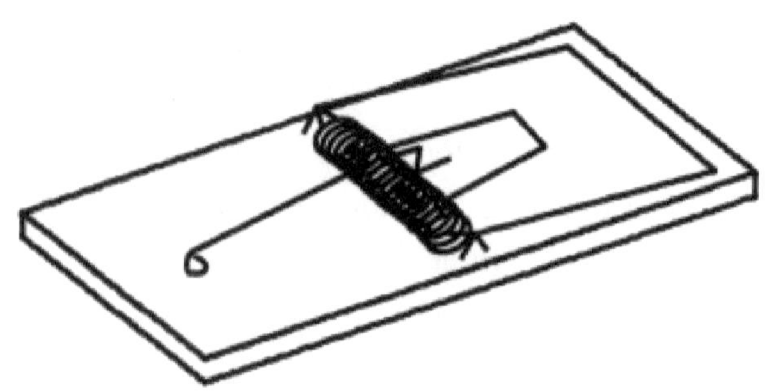

THREE

Millie's parents divorced while we were in eighth grade, and her mom moved to Seattle, which meant Millie also moved to Seattle. I was not happy about that.

I started high school friendless, except for Paula, so I read a lot and listened to the radio like I had back at the funeral home. Books and radio were almost like friends.

Most of my classes were boring, so I would hide a book in my lap to read during the lectures. Most teachers either didn't notice or didn't care, and I was usually able to read a book a day. Paula liked to nap on the ground between my feet during class. When she got bored, she would scale my legs like a rock wall.

We had gotten a cow-box computer from an estate sale, and I used it message Millie whenever I could.

Millie: Hi Bev! how are you doing?
Me: ok I guess

Millie: Me too! I never thought I would like school. how r the boys back home?

Me: what boys?

Millie: like the boys who go to your new school,

Millie: any of them cute?

Me: not really

Me: and Jake is even more of a jerk

Millie: Aw! I miss Jake!

Millie: There are so many cute boys in Seattle, its INSANE.

Me: Cool.

Millie: I even kissed one! Garrett, he's so cute, and he's smart, and he's even good at sports.

I worried that my friend Millie didn't really exist anymore—not how I wanted her to anyway.

————

A few weeks into the school year, we developed a mouse problem in our duplex. Suzie chased them sometimes but never caught any. Paula was scared of them, so she'd hide whenever we saw any.

The mice inspired Bea to move in with some of her friends in Portland. "It's like this place is haunted but with mice!" She had been living at home and going to community college.

I had a lot of trouble falling asleep in high school because I would just think about depressing things. The stuff I heard on the news made more sense to me now. Thirty-two people died at Virginia Tech. California was on fire.

I thought about how our neighbor on the other side of the duplex seemed to get to do whatever he wanted all the time. His life seemed perfect. He went on a whittling kick while I was in high school. No normal person had time to get good at whittling.

I thought about the mice a lot because I could hear them scritching all the time. They were in the walls. My parents put out traps, which worked for some of them. Then a few weeks later, an exterminator came and acted very smart, looking around. She put poison in some places.

Over the next few days, all the of mice disappeared except for one: Mr. Meanie Pants. I named him. He was a regular gray mouse who could talk but often prefered to grunt instead.

The other mice never talked. Mr. Meanie Pants was different. He smelled kind of like gasoline. He never wore pants, which made my name choice a bit ironic. He wore a Hawaiian shirt with red flowers and a khaki backpack full of cilantro. Some mice tried to be cool by riding motorcycles, but Mr. Meanie Pants chose a mini skateboard instead. His skateboard was probably why he hadn't died with all the other mice.

———

One day, as I was walking home past the McDonald's I couldn't afford to stop at anymore, I heard Mr. Meanie Pants say, "Your shoes are untied."

I looked down. They were not even a little untied. I furrowed my brow.

"I said they will be untied soon."

"That's not what you said," I whispered while trying to figure out where he was.

"You'd better tie them."

"They are tied!"

"They won't be, and then you'll trip and break your leg, and your parents will go bankrupt from medical bills."

I gave up and untied my shoes so I could tie them again. This time, I did it tighter and double knotted them.

———

I had watched Ben and Bea go through high school, so I thought I knew what to expect, but it wasn't working out that way for me. Both of them had dated a bit and hung out with friends almost every day. Ben got really good grades and played on the baseball team. Bea played tuba and was on the debate team. I read books by myself and talked to Paula and Mr. Meanie Pants because they were all I had.

Part of the reason I didn't try very hard to date in high school was that no one seemed like more fun to hang out with than Millie. Kissing looked sort of fun, but I didn't want to kiss just any person. I wanted to kiss someone I liked. I liked Paula a lot, but she was too little and scaly.

"And I wouldn't kiss you, because you're gross," Mr. Meanie Pants reminded me. I didn't want to kiss him anyway.

———

Sophomore year, I decided I should at least be somewhat sociable so people wouldn't think I was a total loser. I tried out for a few sports teams. That was what cool people did in high school.

I tried out for track, but while I was doing the one-hundred-meter dash, Mr. Meanie Pants came running out from under the bleachers and tripped me. "You can run, but I can hide!" he blurted as he went past me.

I had enjoyed playing soccer in gym class when I was younger, up until all the other kids learned how to make the ball go up in the air. That was too advanced for me. At the soccer tryout, Mr. Meanie Pants sat on my shoulder and grunted into my ear every time the ball got anywhere close to me. I would always flinch instead of kicking the ball.

I considered trying out for softball, but as I pulled out my pencil to sign up, Mr. Meanie Pants whispered, "It's too bad you're a girl and you can't try out for the real sport."

I ended up joining the newspaper club. They let anybody join because most people didn't want to. Instead of wallowing at home, I wallowed in a musty classroom with Mitchell, Shelby, Tristan, Craig, Dustin, Luis, Richard, Paige, and Jerry.

I drew comics for the paper instead of coming up with random things to write about. Paula helped me come up with ideas for my drawings, and Mr. Meanie Pants did indirectly as well. He inspired the darker ones. My comics were about a refrigerator, and all the food in it would come to life and talk about things. It was a pretty morbid comic because eventually, all the food would get eaten or thrown out. Milk was the main character, but obviously, it was not always the same carton of milk.

"What if you do one with puns about cheese?" Paula suggested.

"That's super overdone. What about you make it so the cheese is for a trap that will tear you in half?" Mr. Meanie Pants suggested.

I thought both of these ideas were pretty dumb.

When I said so, that mouse yelled back, "Well, why don't you burn the whole thing in a dumpster fire, then?"

My next comic was about the food discussing a fire that the new food had seen on the way home from the grocery store. None of them understood what fire was. The only temperature they understood was cold.

My mom pointed out that since I liked drawing, I might be interested in learning about architecture. I did like the idea of drawing useful things, but I was also not that good at drawing.

———

Millie: I MADE THE CHEERLEADING TEAM!

   Me: What?! really?

   Millie: Yea Lindsey said she was going to try out and that I should too

   Millie: and Tory was on the team last year so she was pretty sure she'd be on it again

   Millie: and so I did but I didn't think I was gonna make it

   Millie: BUT THEN I DID MAKE IT! AH!

   Me: Congratulations! I joined the newspaper blub

   Me: club

   Millie: That's so cool, Beverly.

She was number one in my top eight on Myspace, followed by a few of the nerds from the newspaper crew and then some of the popular kids I wished I was friends with. I was number six in Millie's top eight. Her number one was Garrett. He sounded awful to me, but she liked him, I guess. Lindsey was number three, and Tory was number seven. The other spots on her top eight were people I didn't know.

———

One Friday night over winter break, my parents had to pull an all-nighter because they had four funerals scheduled for the next day. Ben had come back from Ann Arbor, and Bea had come over from Portland to visit for a few days. It was starting to snow a little bit, so we all took turns using the computer and hanging out.

We played a round of Settlers of Catan before Ben headed to his old room and Bea headed to our room. It looked like I was going to win because I had a monopoly on sheep, which meant I could make really good trades. Then at the end, it turned out that Bea won because she had the biggest army.

I was hanging out on Myspace for maybe an hour before I looked over at Suzie sleeping on the rug, but then it didn't look like she was breathing. "Suzie?"

Nothing. I walked over and jostled her, but she didn't do anything. Suzie did have some gray hair, but I was still not ready for her to die. It felt like my head was magically floating.

I yelled for Ben. He came out of his room, shirtless with flannel pajama pants. For a few seconds, he just stared at her. He ruffled his hair to make his bedhead look a little less bedhead-like. Then matter-of-factly, he said, "Looks like we'll have to have a funeral."

We woke up Bea to help begin the preparations. Luckily, we didn't have to do all the paperwork that my parents did. We only had to do the fun parts of funeral planning. Bea played the role of Meredith and dug a big hole in our backyard. It was still dark out, so probably no one saw her, but if they did, it must have looked super ominous. We did not have any dog caskets lying around the house, so Ben took a random cardboard box from his room and dumped all the stuff out of it.

When our parents got home, Ben told them, "Well, we've had an interesting evening, but don't worry. We've taken care of everything."

We gathered in the backyard as the sun was coming up. My mom looked like she was about to cry, and my dad looked like he was about to giggle.

Even Paula came to the funeral, but she hid in my pocket the whole time. I could see Mr. Meanie Pants's shadow as he watched from the window of the duplex, and I could faintly hear him grunting throughout the service.

Ben gave the eulogy. "Tonight, we say goodbye too soon to Suzette Fuzzers Blevins. Life does not always go how you expect it, but Suzie lived like she didn't know it was ever going to end. She'd always stop to smell the poop or the fire hydrant, no matter how hard we tried to stop her. She was never one to play fetch. Whenever I'd try, she'd just stare at me with a look that said, 'You threw it. You go get it.' We will all miss her. She was a good dog. Good dog."

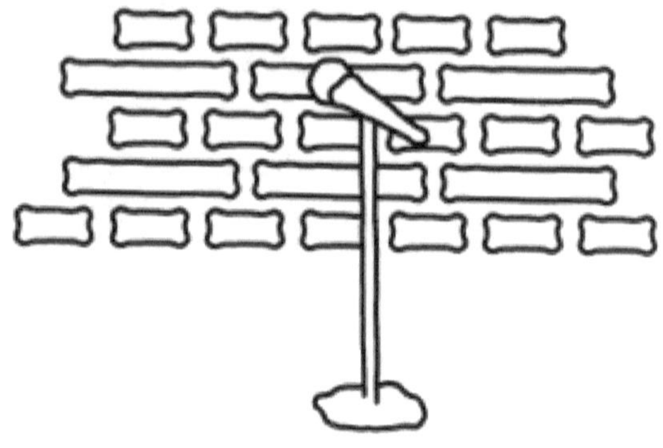

FOUR

Ben's wedding was beautiful. Everyone looked happy. It was one of the only times I ever wore a dress.

Mr. Meanie Pants sat on my shoulder the whole time, grunt-whispering to me. "This is never going to happen for you. You don't even have friends. How on earth are you ever going to trick someone into marrying you? You're attractive enough not to be ugly, but that's about it. Oh, that kiss was so romantic. That must be a nice thing to experience. And doesn't she look so natural in that dress? It's like she was just born to wear it. Born for great things. How is Ben so smart and good at things? You two are supposedly related, right?"

After the ceremony, one of our cousins from Montana suggested that we should all get together more often because it was good to see everybody. My dad chimed in. "Yes it would be sad if the only time we saw each other was for weddings and funerals."

————

I vaguely considered college but decided against it. I wanted to try standup comedy, which you didn't have to go to school for. I wanted to be funny like the people on *Wait, Wait, Don't Tell Me.*

My brother and sister were already on the road to conquering every other measure of success. Ben was hoping to be a father soon and was working toward his PhD in medieval history. Bea was marching or protesting something or other almost every week to try to make the world a better place. She took some classes at Portland State, mostly political science, but she never got a degree. I felt like I had to find my own thing, and comedy felt right.

I wrote some attempts at jokes about food and current events, and I went to an open mic at the Brody. I put my name on the list, and then I sat in one of the armless green chairs and waited.

There were a few audience members, but it was mostly comedians. There were fake candles on all the tables, and the stool on the stage was so old it was being held together with duct tape. I imagined Steve Martin learning to be funny in a place like this. By the time I went up, the real audience members had trickled away, but it didn't really matter because once I was onstage, the lights blinded me, and I couldn't see anybody. Nobody laughed, but they clapped for me at the end.

Some of the things that the comics said were really more ideas than jokes, or it turned out the jokes were more funny in the comic's head. My favorite local comedian was Ravi. He was quite cute for a boy. He was also under twenty-one, so we ran into each other a lot at the open mics that allowed minors. He liked to do lots of poop and fart jokes, but his were funnier than most of the ones I heard.

———————

Me: Hey Millie, how's it going?
     She never answered.

———————

I got a boring job at an office so society and my parents wouldn't think of me as a loser who made no money. My office job was my "day job," as artistic people liked to say. Everyone who worked in the office was obsessed with coffee. One day, the coffee maker was broken, and nothing got done until Cheryl went on a Starbucks run.

Every office had a Cheryl. Our Cheryl wore sweaters with woodland creatures on them and was very chatty and sociable, always asking people how their weekend went and remembering their names and stuff. She had the idea to go to Starbucks, and when she got back, everyone welcomed her like she was an entire high school football team entering the field.

One day, I went to grab my coffee cup from the break room, and it wasn't there. My mug used to belong to some guy named Eugene, and it had a photograph of him in his golfing outfit. There was an almost-full pot of fresh coffee, but I had no way to drink it. I took a deep breath, but smelling was not the same as tasting. I wanted it in my mouth. I could have just grabbed one of the other mugs in there, but I didn't want an endless cycle of people using other people's mugs. I had a mug.

I walked back to my desk to get a file folder to carry with me so I'd look casual. I meandered through the office until I noticed my mug sitting on Cheryl's desk. Everything else got blurry, and all I could focus on was my mug. Maybe she thought all the mugs in the break room were communal, but that one wasn't.

"Hi, Beverly. How was your weekend?" she asked when she saw me hovering.

"Oh, it was good. How was yours?" I looked at my mug but pretended it was just a regular mug and not the thing I wanted most.

Everyone had a mailbox in the break room. Later, I checked Cheryl's mail and was happy to see she had a letter in there. I added it to my pile of mail and took it back to my cube. I waited a couple of hours until she got up to go to the bathroom. Then I dashed over with her letter and set it on her keyboard as I grabbed my mug.

I wanted to run but knew that would draw too much attention to myself, so I leisurely headed back to my cube. When Cheryl returned, I could hear her asking Kathy if she knew where her coffee was.

"No, but maybe Beverly knows. I saw her go in there."

"Beverly?" Cheryl asked over the cubicle walls. "Why were you in my cube?"

"Oh, um, some of your mail ended up in my mailbox. I was just dropping it off." I quietly hid the mug behind my computer monitor in case she was about to come over, but she accepted my answer. She left to retrace her steps instead.

"You're such a wimp," Mr. Meanie Pants said.

I noticed the lipstick her lips had left my coffee cup. I drank the coffee anyway.

—————

I had to upgrade Paula to a more adult-looking lunch box to hang out in. In high school, the hard plastic one was deemed cool, but now it drew too much attention. I switched to a boring insulated navy-blue one with a velcro flap on top. It was probably more comfortable for Paula anyway since it was soft. She hung out in there most of the day while I was working. Whenever someone did something dumb, like, "Oh no! I forgot to save what I was working on, and now it's gone!" I could hear Paula giggling in my lunch box.

Once I had saved up a chunk of money, I also bought an e-reader. That made reading much easier for Paula. Otherwise, she would have needed four of her to read a book: two to hold it open, one to turn the pages, and one to actually read it.

—————

One summer weekend, I had planned on going for a long hike in the park because hiking was as different from working in an office as you could get. Mr. Meanie Pants must have known what I was planning, because he sat just outside my bedroom window, smoking cigars. He smoked so many that the whole Portland area was filled with smoke.

Being outside became even more unpleasant than being stuck inside, so I climbed up into bed with some bourbon and wrote jokes instead. The best joke I came up with was pretending that literally all the squirrels were having birthday parties at the same time and that was why it was so smoky. I knew that wasn't true, but Paula agreed it was a fun idea.

———

I was staying home sick one day and relaxing on the bottom bunk. I did a lot of wallowing during this sickness, but I enjoyed it. I was proud of how pathetic I was. Every time I opened my mouth to talk, I didn't know what my voice was going to sound like. I imagined this was what it was like to be a pubescent boy. If I had been like that in middle school, Millie probably would have thought I was super hot.

My nose was quite runny, so I reached over to pull out a tissue, but instead of paper, I felt fur. I jumped. Mr. Meanie Pants was sitting on my now empty tissue box.

"What?" I mumbled." Where are all my tissues?"

He cackled gruntily. "They're gone. Just like how you made my whole family disappear," he said, suddenly serious. Paula peeked her head up out of her bedroom drawer. She was not very confrontational, but she did like to feel involved.

Mr. Meanie laughed before continuing, "I've taken them! I've taken them all and torn them to shreds and left them for birds to find and turn into nests."

"What? That's littering," I said.

"Not to the birds, it's not. Are you saying you'd rather have a dry nose and homeless birds instead of a wet nose and homeful birds? I think the birds are more important than you."

I was too sleepy to argue. I wiped my nose on my sleeve and fell asleep.

FIVE

I went on a date with a woman I'd met at a bar, like a stereotypical person. We went out to Casa Daisy to eat some Italian food, the most romantic food. This woman, Laura, seemed pretty cool, and we were eating quite a bit of linguini. She offered to pay, which was why we went to a nicer place than McDonald's.

Paula knew to stay in my pocket or at home when I was on a date, but Mr. Meanie Pants was not so polite. There must have been mouseholes in all the places I went, because he always seemed to magically show up. I wanted to be the roadrunner in our relationship, but it felt like I was the dumb coyote.

I'd heard that mice were extra good at hearing because they were so small that they could feel sound vibrations all over their bodies. Maybe that was why he could always find me. His whole body was basically an ear.

On this date, I watched as he skateboarded under our table and tickled Laura's feet. She was wearing sandals. I kept forgetting to breathe while I watched him. Her feet must not have been very sensitive, because she didn't seem to feel it.

"What are you looking at?" she asked.

I had been staring in the direction of her feet for quite a while. I told the truth and said a mouse was under the table, and she screamed and knocked her plate of pasta onto the floor when she flailed her arms. The sauce got everywhere.

Everyone started yelling for napkins, and as the waiters tried to bring them, they slipped in the sauce that was all over the floor, creating an even bigger mess. One of the waiters dropped his tray with plates of fettuccine, ravioli, and tortellini.

Of course, this was a pretty fancy restaurant, so they had all been wearing white shirts with black bow ties to begin with. Now the whole restaurant was turning red. Mr. Meanie Pants laughed and laughed. Paula also thought it was kind of funny when I told her about it later. I never heard from Laura again.

―――――

When I turned twenty-one, I could perform anywhere. The first time I went to the Boiler Room, I discovered that you could get a beer for just a dollar, so I had a couple before I went up.

"Hoagie you all doing?" I asked the audience. It felt like they did not even realize comedy was happening.

I plowed on until, in the middle of my favorite cereal joke, I heard a small voice between people ordering drinks, shooting pool, and chatting. The voice was mocking me, but no one else seemed to hear it. "Hey! Hey! We want a comedian! Not a highway median!"

Then I saw him perched on one of the lights, most of which were tinted red. Mr. Meanie Pants. I could just make out his silhouette. I couldn't escape him.

My mind became mushy spaghetti, and I couldn't think of any jokes except for the ones I had told already. "That doesn't even make sense!" I yelled to the rafters.

The audience all froze in silence.

I had to save this somehow. "Airline food, right? It doesn't make any sense. How do they get so much food so high up?"

A soft chuckle.

"Real comedians don't joke about food!" Mr. Meanie Pants squeaked.

He was getting to me. Paula was writhing around in my pocket. I could tell she was disappointed in me because she shook a little bit and then went limp, like a deep sigh against my thigh. The host of the show gave me the light and made a Jim Halpert face.

———

A few days after the fiasco at Casa Daisy, I got a text message from a random number with a 208 area code, asking if I wanted to do a comedy show in Boise. I assumed there was no comedy in Boise because people in Idaho were incapable of laughing. They just dealt with potatoes, which was an important job but made the state no fun to visit.

This had to be another one of Mr. Meanie Pants's tricks. I should have just ignored him, but I decided to humor him for a little bit.

Me: *Yeah, right, potato man. I know you don't know how to laugh.*

208 number: *Well, actually, I do. I run a comedy show. You can just say no if your not interested.*

Me: *Ha! Yeah right, Mr. Meanie Pants!*

208 number: *What did you call me?*

Me: *You heard me. Your name! You can take your "comedy show" and make a piña colada with it!*

After I sent the text, I realized I should have picked a more disgusting drink, like a Bloody Mary.

208 number: *You'll never work in Boise again!*

Me: *Who would want to?*

Then I noticed Mr. Meanie Pants was sitting a few feet away and laughing at me. He wasn't the one texting. At least I did not burn actual bridges, because then I would be in jail.

— — — — —

Since I was a comedian, I thought it would be fun to start a podcast with somebody. Ravi was the obvious person to do it with. I thought it would be cool to hang out at fast food restaurants and talk about it like it was super fancy. We could even have other comedians on as guests, and we could let them pick their favorite fast food places.

If we went to McDonald's, we might say, "Wow, these salads are divine."

"Lots of food is finger-licking good, but I suppose it is true that this food is as well."

"These fries are not as famous, but I would argue that they are tastier," we might say at Burger King.

"That is a stupid idea," Mr. Meanie Pants said. I figured he was probably right.

———

A few months later, I got a message on Facebook. It was someone asking me to perform in Cincinnati, the comedy capital of Ohio. I felt famous. I imagined this could be my big break. I was hesitant, but it felt real, so I went along with it. I figured if Mr. Meanie Pants was messing with me, he would have come up with something more creative.

On my way to Cincinnati, I attempted to go through security at the airport, but when they sent my bag through the scanner, I could see a mouse skeleton on the screen. Paula had come with me, but she was smart enough not to get caught. She waited until no one was looking and then scurried under the scanners.

I kept forgetting to breathe, and that made me start shaking. The TSA person must have noticed because she said, "Is everything all right?"

And I tried to say yes, but it came out as a whisper, and maybe she didn't hear me. So then she got suspicious of my bag. She looked closer on the scanner and saw the mouse skeleton.

"I'm gonna need you to step aside, Miss." She brought my bag over to the investigating table and unzipped it. She was short, so she stood on a stepstool. I was bracing myself for Mr. Meanie Pants to jump out and spit in her face or something.

With her gloved hand, she pulled a dead mouse out of my bag. It wasn't Mr. Meanie Pants. I could tell because this mouse was naked. No khaki backpack or Hawaiian shirt. Sometimes a mouse is a just mouse.

"Why was this mouse in your bag?" she asked me.

"I don't know."

"Are there drugs inside this mouse?"

"No."

She called to one of her coworkers, "I'm going to need a drug-sniffing dog over here."

"We'll have to call and have them send one over," her coworker yelled back.

"That's fine." She thought this was fine, but I did not because I knew my flight would be taking off in just under an hour. I glanced around to see if I could find Paula, but she must have been hiding.

The TSA person continued interrogating me. "Is that dog going to find drugs in this mouse?"

"No."

"Why were you trying to bring this mouse with you, then? Is there a weapon inside this mouse?"

"No. I wasn't trying—"

"If I dissect this mouse will I find cocaine?"

"No," I said.

"Oh, so you're saying there is heroin in this mouse?"

"No, there are no drugs in that mouse."

"We'll see about that."

Maybe this was Mr. Meanie Pants's way of getting back at me for being involved in killing his family all those years ago, I thought. Or perhaps we had another mouse problem in the duplex, and I hadn't noticed because I'd been so excited about Cincinnati.

We stood there for forty minutes before the dog came and was uninterested in the dead mouse. Once the TSA let me go, I ran to my gate but it was too late. I wasn't going to make it to the show.

SIX

Luckily, the comedy club was willing to reschedule me to another week. I was tempted to say no because it was when I was supposed to go to the family reunion in Montana, but it seemed rude to try to change it. I had never performed in a big city so far away. This could be my big shot. Plus, I saw my parents all the time since I was still living with them.

When I packed my backpack for the second attempt at the trip, I was very careful to make sure there weren't any mice in it. I checked everywhere inside it. I even smelled it. Not even a hint of gasoline or cilantro! I zipped it up super quickly.

I knew that shortly after I left for the airport, Bea, Ben, and his wife were going to meet at the duplex. Then they, along with our parents, would get on a train to ride to the reunion together. They'd said it would be nice to hang out together and see the scenery.

I hadn't seen Mr. Meanie Pants for a few days, and it had been quite nice. Odd, but nice. Maybe I was done with him for good, I thought. This trip, there was no mouse skeleton on the scanner.

I got to Cincinnati a bit earlier than I needed to, so I relaxed in my hotel room for a bit. I flipped through the channels. I got tired of sitting alone in my room, so I went to a bar near the comedy club to grab a bourbon before the show. I got my notebook out and thought through the jokes I was going to do. They seemed pretty funny.

One of the TVs in the bar was showing a train crash, and the other was showing a baseball game. Neither was that interesting to me. The news was sad, and sports were boring to watch.

After another drink of bourbon, I signed my receipt with impressively good cursive. I'd discovered that drinking made my cursive a lot better, which hadn't been helpful in elementary school but was useful to me now as an adult. I thought maybe one day I'd open a calligraphy store, and whenever my writing wasn't looking so good, I'd open another beer.

I left the bar and walked over to the comedy club. The theme of the show was alternative up-and-coming comedians. They must have considered me up-and-coming.

It was one of the best sets I'd ever had. The audience cheered before I even said anything. They laughed at the setups to my jokes, and I only had time for half of the jokes I'd planned. The audience probably thought I was vegetarian because I didn't do any of my meat-related jokes. The show felt magical compared to performing for three people at midnight at the Brody. I kept expecting Mr. Meanie Pants to show up and ruin everything, but he never did.

I went back to the hotel room and tried to call my parents on their cell phone to let them know how it had gone. It was earlier where they were because of the different time zones. They didn't answer, which wasn't that unusual. They had the phone mostly just for emergencies. Perhaps they did not have reception. I was hungry, so I went downstairs to the hotel bar to grab some food and a beer. Then I went upstairs and fell asleep.

At about four in the morning, I got a call on my cell phone. It was my cousin who I hadn't seen for about fifteen years. He was frantic. I didn't know how he'd gotten my number. It surprised me to hear his voice sounding so low. He was saying words really fast, and I couldn't understand all of it. "You need to come home... crash... gone."

I was not completely awake, and I was still a bit buzzed, but I understood that my family had never made it to Montana. I hung up on my cousin, which was rude, but I couldn't listen to him anymore. I was scared my brain was going to implode. It felt like that ride at amusement parks that didn't have seatbelts because it just spun so fast you'd get stuck to the side instead of falling out.

I sat in bed for a few minutes, staring at the curtains. I tried to remember what color they were. Dark blue was my guess, but it was dark, so I couldn't really tell. I could have turned the light on, but I didn't want to. Curtain color was not important at a time like this.

I ran to the bathroom and threw up and threw up again. It felt impossible to throw up enough, even though nothing else was coming up. Once I was convinced my body was empty, I threw on some non-pajamas. I had to get out of that hotel room.

I ran down the sidewalk and down Old Pfeiffer road. I had to get away from the place where this could happen. I'd never learned horrible things like this at home.

The houses at the end of the long driveways still had their lights off. I ran to the end of the street, past all the trees and grass. The sun was starting to come up.

I'd thought life was generally a happy place, but it was looking like I'd been wrong. Now all the sad people I had seen in the funeral home made sense. I tried to talk to Paula about the accident, but she disappeared that day and stayed gone for several weeks afterward. I knew she hadn't been on the train because she'd been with me in Cincinnati.

———

I forgot to go to work on Monday. I didn't want to have to explain to them why I'd forgotten, so I never went back. The idea of Cheryl asking about my weekend felt horrible. Sitting in my cubicle didn't seem that different from being in a coffin.

I considered talking to Ravi, but I didn't want him to try to date me out of pity or anything. I didn't really have Millie to talk to anymore either. I wished I was still close to her. Really, I wanted to talk to Ben.

———

Even though I didn't feel like it, I had to get things done. At first, I tried to figure out how I could sell our half of the duplex. Then I found out we'd only been renting it from our neighbor on the other side of the duplex, which meant I just had to leave. There was no way I could afford the rent on my own.

With some help from Meredith, I sorted through things and sold whatever I didn't want to keep in a garage sale. It was really an estate sale, but I didn't like calling it that. The couch I'd sat on my whole life sold for twenty-five dollars. Our wine glasses sold for a buck apiece.

I collected the few things that I wanted and put them in the hearse. Our hearse was pretty old, but it worked. I had to live somewhere. I grabbed my moose, Quentin. I grabbed a bottle of bourbon. I took my twin mattress off the bunk bed and put it in the back of the vehicle.

The hearse was not fancy enough to come with a shower, so I chipped away at my garage-sale money and bought a gym membership. Meredith also helped get the funeral home ready to put on the market. The hardest room to clean out was my old playroom. I took my drawings off the wall and put them in the hearse's glove box.

It felt too quiet. I couldn't hear the rustling of my mom working. I couldn't hear my dad speaking calmly and patiently with the customers. The only thing I could still hear was Meredith humming softly, almost like she'd done back when she was digging.

Before we put the funeral home on the market, Meredith helped me plan the funeral to be held there. We did one big celebration of life for all of them since the event was mostly for my benefit. It was a somewhat small gathering—a few family friends from town and most of our family from Montana. I was still in a fog, but I remember lots of hugs. Dennis came, and I tried to comfort him as best I could, but he was pretty upset about losing his friend. Meredith did eulogies for everyone, and it was really beautiful, but I didn't really pay attention. It felt like I was in a weird dream. After the service, everyone took turns checking on me and being all awkward when they tried to talk to me. I wouldn't have known what to say either. I remembered Ben's eulogy for Suzie. Her funeral felt like a joke now.

———

I had to have been sleeping, but it felt like I was awake. I was standing in the wilderness of Idaho near some train tracks. I saw a train coming, and I knew it was the one my family was on. Everything looked okay, but I knew the crash was about to happen. I looked desperately for something I could do to stop it. There was nothing to do.

"Your shoes are untied."

I looked down at Mr. Meanie Pants, who was standing next to my clearly tied shoes. "They're not."

Crash. I had missed it. I'd been looking at my shoes. It was too late. I looked up, and everything was still, like one of the pictures I'd seen on the news. Train cars were tipped over and crunched. There was smoke. I heard sirens off in the distance.

In another dream, I was snoozing and could hear my dad in the other room yelling for me to wake up. "Bev! Beverly, come on! It's time to go to school."

When I woke up, I was alone. I grabbed the bourbon from near Paula's lunch box and took a big swig.

———

I went for a walk by myself. I liked to go for walks when I was feeling down. I imagined that because walking brought the heart rate up, that meant you would feel down more efficiently so you could get back to feeling up faster. It sounded reasonable in my head. If I had become a doctor instead of a comedian, I would know useful stuff like that.

I walked by a playground, which was mostly full of children, but there was one person about the same age as me on the merry-go-round. She wasn't exactly playing. She was using a selfie stick. She would spin around and pretend to be having an amazing time. Then she would stop and analyze the pictures.

The whole thing felt faker than Disneyland. *What's the point of looking happy if you're just pretending?*

Suddenly, I got very angry. I imagined Mr. Meanie Pants tickling the train conductor or playing peekaboo, distracting him when he should have been focused on driving the train. If not that, maybe he had found a tiny pickaxe and worked to break apart the track. I imagined him cackling as he sang, "I've Been Working on the Railroad."

People didn't just die like that. Mr. Meanie Pants had to be involved.

I walked to the Fred Meyer. It had been renovated, so I didn't know where things were. I found the produce section and stared at the displays. I wanted to crawl under the nectarines and stay there for the rest of the day, but I was too big.

John Denver's "Leaving on a Jet Plane" was playing softly, and I pictured Ben sitting in his room, ignoring me, while he listened to it.

I was walking by the freezer with ice cream sandwiches when Paula said, "Those look so tasty."

"I don't have any money," I said.

"That's okay. Just take one. No one is watching."

"That's not nice."

"But what if you took it out and left it on a shelf somewhere? It would melt and be worthless. A better option is taking it and eating it."

That sounded reasonable, and I was hungry so I put it in my pocket and left the store. No one seemed to notice. Once I was down the street, I opened it and took a bite. It almost felt like a hug but on the inside.

———

I got a phone call from Millie a few weeks after the crash. It would have been a reasonable time to tell her about it, but it never came up. She could have asked, "Hey, did all of your family die in a horrible train crash?" but she didn't, so I didn't mention it. It was so nice to hear a voice from the past that I didn't want to spoil the pleasantness of the phone call, but it ended up being a sad phone call anyway. She had called to tell me that Jake, that annoying boy from elementary school, had died. He had cancer or alcohol poisoning or some tragic thing like that.

She sounded very upset, and she was worried I would be as well. I think to her he was the boy who got away. Now she for sure was never going to be with him. I was upset, but not about Jake dying. The upsetting thing was that it reminded me that everyone was going to die. Months passed, and I still never felt upset about Jake dying.

SEVEN

After a couple of months of being in a fog, I started going out to open mics as often as I could to distract myself. Paula would show up there sometimes. I ran into Ravi a lot also, which was nice. Then one night, I was watching him perform, and he did a joke about his boyfriend. It didn't seem made-up. It sounded like he really had a boyfriend. This put a serious kink in my plan to maybe marry him one day.

Sometimes I stayed in Portland because it was familiar, but I often went on road trips to perform stand-up in other places. I would drive until I saw a town with a silly name, and then I'd stop and try to do comedy there if I could. I figured people who lived in places with names like Sammamish or Puyallup must have a reasonable sense of humor.

I realized since my family was all dead, I could make whatever jokes about them that I wanted, and no one could complain. My first attempt didn't go so well: "My mom is always misplacing things, but not anymore because she's dead." I stared at the audience, willing them to laugh, but it didn't work. Paula laughed sympathetically from my pocket.

————

As I was driving around, I also kept my eye out for college towns. Those were the best places to find parties, which always had lots of food. If I was in the mood for a fancier party, I'd grab some Two-Buck Chuck on my way. Otherwise, I'd stop at a Walgreens and grab a sixpack of Big Flats.

When I found a hopping party, I'd walk in like I belonged there. If anyone questioned me, I'd tell them I was Jessica's friend. I didn't have a friend named Jessica or really any friends besides Paula—I'd just made her up. I brought alcohol so people wouldn't assume I was just coming to the party to eat their food and drink their drinks.

One time, in Rexburg, I told this girl I was Jessica's friend, and she said, "What? I'm Jessica."

So I said, "No, I'm friends with the other Jessica. You're not my Jessica." I laughed awkwardly.

"What other Jessica?"

"She has long hair."

"Um, okay."

I was worried she was going to go tell the host I was just some random person, so I snuck away as smoothly as I could.

————

A while later, I finagled my way onto a show at the comedy club in Walla Walla. After the show, I drank quite a bit of bourbon and beer while I was hanging out with the local comedians and fans. They weren't fans of me but, rather, were fans of sitting in dark places and listening to sadness that was trying to pose as humor. When I got tired of hanging out, I left for my hearse.

I'd felt a little dorky driving around in the hearse all the time, so I covered the back of it with bumper stickers, thinking that it made me more hip. I'd chosen the most random collection of bumper stickers I could find to make the hearse feel more homey. As I was walking back to my hearse to go to sleep, I looked up and saw Mr. Meanie Pants towering above everything. He was taller than most of the buildings in Walla Walla, which would not have been impressive if he'd been a building, but since he was a mouse, it was super impressive. He was terrorizing the whole town. People were just minding their own business, though. He was being such a jerk to all these smallish-town people, but none of them were paying attention.

"Look at that mouse!" I screamed. People glanced at me quickly but then looked away. I got no credit for trying to help them. *Stomp, stomp, stomp.* Mr. Meanie Pants kept looking down at passersby and mocking them. He was just stomping around and yelling. I was afraid he was going to give people the bubonic plague.

"Did you fall in a vat of paint, or do you just really love green clothes?" he said to one person.

I tried to defend those perfectly nice people, but it was no use. "Let's just go back to the hearse and relax," Paula pleaded from my pocket. Why was no one else freaking out like I was? I woke up later with an awful headache.

———

On Thanksgiving, I went to Shari's by myself. I felt rich because I had made fifty-eight dollars at a comedy show in Troutdale. Some of the other people there, like me, were eating alone. I wondered why we all didn't sit together, but none of us looked at each other.

There was an older couple, each having a slice of pie. The man had lemon meringue, and the woman had marionberry. They were watching people walking by out the window and commenting on them. "That lady is only wearing a sweatshirt."

"It could snow any minute."

More bites of pie.

"I think it's not supposed to snow until Wednesday."

"That would be pretty, wouldn't it?"

More pie.

"That guy's having a heck of a time getting into that parking spot."

"He's coming in at the wrong angle. That's the problem."

"It would've been easier if he was coming at it from the other direction."

"If he drove down farther, there are lots of easy spots, but he doesn't see them, I guess."

My parents would never get to be that couple.

———

"Why did this happen?"

Paula peeked out from her lunch box. "Everything happens for a reason."

"So I'm being punished?" I adjusted my pillow and stared at the hearse's ceiling.

"No, I'm just saying there's some reason you haven't figured out yet. They're in a better place."

"I doubt it," I said. "They all seemed so happy. I don't know if I'll ever be happy again."

"You will. What doesn't kill you makes you stronger."

I rolled over and closed my eyes.

—————

A few months later, I drove up to see Mount St. Helens. I got out of the hearse and stared. I tried to imagine what the mountain used to look like but couldn't. Paula walked around and looked at the scenery.

"Why did you come see a broken mountain?" Mr. Meanie Pants asked.

I laughed. "It's pretty. It's not broken."

"It is broken."

I never thought this would happen, but in some ways, I found myself enjoying spending time with Mr. Meanie Pants more than with Paula. Maybe Mr. Meanie Pants was more realistic. Paula was just happy and positive all the time, but Mr. Meanie Pants understood how things were.

"It's me that's broken," I said. "I don't have a job. I'm chronically single. Maybe I should become a dishwasher."

"So you're giving up on your dream?" He was sitting in the cupholder next to my bed. Most hearses didn't come with cupholders in the back, but my mom had installed them to be funny. They were the kind that you pushed into the squishy part of the window. They came in quite handy once I was living back there.

"I don't even know what my dream is. There are so many things that sound reasonable."

"Well, right now, you're an unemployed comedian living in a hearse," he said.

"You're a mini rat who rides a skateboard and doesn't make any positive contributions to the world."

"Sucks to be us."

"Nobody likes me," I sang.

"Everybody hates me," he sang.

"Guess I'll go eat worms."

We both laughed.